RAVI'S ROAR

TOM PERCIVAL

BLOOMSBURY
CHILDREN'S BOOKS

LONDON   OXFORD   NEW YORK   NEW DELHI   SYDNEY

Ravi was the youngest
and the smallest
in his family.

KIRAN

JAYA
ANIL

RAVI

Everyone was bigger than him . . .

Even Biscuits the dog!

Most of the time, being the
smallest was great . . .

But sometimes, just *sometimes*, it wasn't.

One day, Ravi and his family went on a picnic.
There was a race to the train and
guess who came last?
Ravi.

Everyone else got a comfy seat but Ravi had
to squash in with Dad and Biscuits.

Then Biscuits made a bad smell.

When everyone got to the park,
they played hide-and-seek.

It was meant to be fun but
Ravi couldn't find *anyone*.

At the adventure playground,
the monkey bars
were too **high**.

The **gaps** between the logs were too **wide**.

And, when Ravi wanted to go
on the BIG slide, the man said,
"Sorry son, you're too small."

Ravi got *so* cross
that his face turned red,
but then Dad said, "Come on,
let's get an ice cream!"

Everybody ran off and guess who came last? Ravi. And *then*, when Ravi went to get *his* ice cream . . .

there was NONE left!

Well, that *really* did it . . .

Ravi was FURIOUS!

He growled . . .

and **a stripy tail** popped out from the back of his shorts.

Then . . .

he sprouted two **furry ears**, sharp, **pointy teeth** and stripy **orange fur!**

Ravi had turned into
a TIGER!

The tiger took a huge,
deep breath and then . . .

Ravi's brother looked a bit nervous
and handed the tiger his ice cream.

When the tiger went to sit down there were
no benches free so he ROARED . . .

and *everybody* got out of the way.

It was GREAT
being a tiger!

The tiger did *all* the
things that Ravi couldn't.

He swung across the monkey bars.
He leapt across the logs.

He even
slid down
the
BIG
slide!

Nobody dared
to say NO . . .

So the tiger went

WILD!

He roared and growled and did *exactly* what he wanted.

But soon he found that *nobody* wanted to play with him.

Suddenly the tiger felt **a** bit sad
and nowhere near as cross.

In fact, he couldn't *quite* remember what had
made him so angry in the first place.

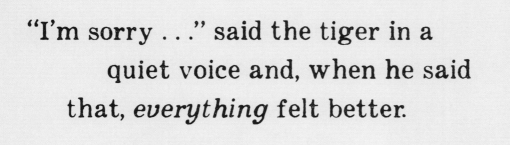

"I'm sorry . . ." said the tiger in a
quiet voice and, when he said
that, *everything* felt better.

"That's okay," said Dad.
"Well done for saying sorry!"

Then, without even realising,
Ravi became a boy once more.

And that was the last time that
Ravi ever turned into a tiger.

Although every
now and then . . .

he did have a *bit* of a growl!

For Vijay, Mila and Indie

BLOOMSBURY CHILDREN'S BOOKS
Bloomsbury Publishing Plc
50 Bedford Square, London, WC1B 3DP, UK

BLOOMSBURY, BLOOMSBURY CHILDREN'S BOOKS and the Diana logo are trademarks of Bloomsbury Publishing Plc

First published in Great Britain by Bloomsbury Publishing Plc

Text and illustrations copyright © Tom Percival 2019

Tom Percival has asserted his rights under the Copyright, Designs and Patents Act, 1988, to be identified as the Author/Illustrator of this work

A catalogue record for this book is available from the British Library

ISBN 978 1 4088 9217 6 (HB)
ISBN 978 1 4088 9218 3 (PB)
ISBN 978 1 4088 9216 9 (eBook)

5 7 9 10 8 6 4

Printed and bound in China by Leo Paper Products, Heshan, Guangdong
All papers used by Bloomsbury Publishing Plc are natural, recyclable products from wood grown in well managed forests.
The manufacturing processes conform to the environmental regulations of the country of origin.

To find out more about our authors and books visit www.bloomsbury.com and sign up for our newsletters